NATHAN'S SECRET

N. Geraldine Plunkett

Beth Gallo, Illustrator

Brethren Press

Nathan's Secret

Copyright © 2000 N. Geraldine Plunkett

Published by Brethren Press, 1451 Dundee Avenue, Elgin, IL 60120

All scripture quotations in this manuscript are from the King James Version of the Bible. The hymn "Guide Me, O Thou Great Jehovah" was written by William Williams, 1717-1791. The letter quoted in the manuscript was written by Henry M. Garst to Ann G. Garst February 23, 1865. The original letter is in the possession of N. Geraldine Plunkett, great-granddaughter of Henry M. Garst, Roanoke, Virginia.

04 03 02 01 00   5 4 3 2 1

Library of Congress Cataloging in Publication Data

Plunkett, N. Geraldine, 1925-
    Nathan's secret / N. Geraldine Plunkett ; Beth Gallo, illustrator.
        p. cm.
    Summary: Following his religious principles as a Brethren, Nathan's father goes into hiding in order not to fight with the Confederate Army but he risks being found when he saves the life of a Union soldier.
    ISBN 0-87178-029-1 (pbk.)
    1. Garst, Henry,—Juvenile fiction. 2. Virginia—History—Civil War, 1861-1865—Juvenile fiction. [Garst, Henry,—Fiction. 2. Virginia—History—Civil War, 1861-1865—Fiction. 3. United States—History—Civil War, 1861-1865—Fiction. 4. Church of the Brethren—Fiction.] I. Gallo, Beth, 1961-ill. II. Title.

PZ7.P737 Nat 2000
[Fic]—dc21

                                                        00-050777

CONTENTS

Dear Readers,

When you read a story, do you wonder if it's true? Did the people in the story really live? Did the events actually happen?

Henry and Ann Garst were real people. They lived in Roanoke County, Virginia. At the time of the Civil War, they had three sons, Nathan, Marshall, and Monroe.

There were two battles in Roanoke County during the Civil War. My grandmother told me stories about those battles—stories that her parents told her. There are also many written records about those battles.

We know where Henry Garst went during the war and why he went there. He wrote about those things in two letters that I still have.

This story started with facts about the Garst family, the Peters Creek Church, and the Civil War. To those facts, I added some fictional neighbors for the Garsts. I made Nathan older than he really was. Then I created actions, conversation, and details to build a story that might have happened—a story that is historical fiction.

—*N. Geraldine Plunkett*

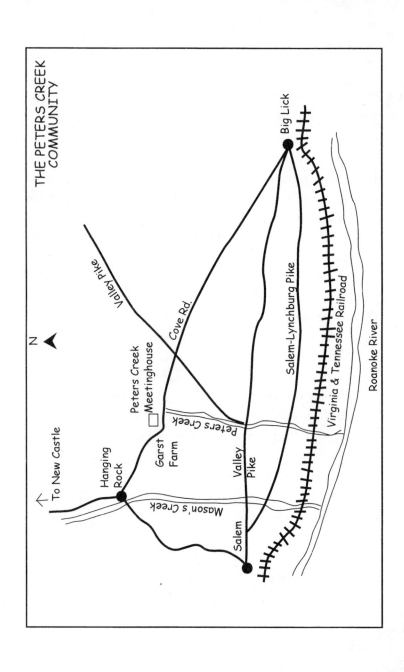

THE PETERS CREEK COMMUNITY

N

To New Castle

Hanging Rock

Valley Pike

Peters Creek Meetinghouse

Garst Farm

Cove Rd.

Mason's Creek

Peters Creek

Valley Pike

Salem

Salem-Lynchburg Pike

Big Lick

Virginia & Tennessee Railroad

Roanoke River

CHAPTER 1

Coward or Man of Peace?

 Dark clouds hid the mountain tops around the Roanoke Valley. The December air was chilly and damp. This kind of day makes you think something unpleasant is going to happen, thought Nathan Garst as he hurried toward the schoolhouse. But the boys in the schoolyard were not thinking about the weather. With sticks resting on their shoulders like muskets, they advanced toward an imaginary foe, singing as they marched. Their voices drifted toward Nathan.

*In Dixie land, I'll take my stand
to live or die in Dixie.*

War was tearing the United States apart. The South was fighting the North. Some said the war was about freeing the slaves. Others said it was about individual states rebelling against the United States government. There were other reasons for the fighting, too. Nathan's papa said that war was not the way to settle matters.

The South was sometimes called Dixie. Virginia was a part of the South. The Southern states wanted to rebel against the North and declare themselves a separate country. It was plain that the boys in the schoolyard thought of themselves as rebels fighting for Dixie against the Yankee soldiers from the North.

No matter why the North and South were angry with one another. Nathan's papa said that war was not the way to settle matters. Nathan's papa said that Brethren boys should not play soldier. But today Nathan saw some Brethren boys marching with their pretend guns along with the other boys.

Most of the children at school had brothers, fathers, uncles, or cousins in the Southern army. Nathan's friend Richard had an older brother who joined the Dixie Grays more than two years ago. He had been fighting in northern Virginia. Nathan also had two unmarried uncles in the Southern army. When the Southern army began to enroll married men, his friend Martin's father, Friedrick Speagle, had been among the first ones ordered to report for duty.

Martin also had an uncle in the army—the Union army. Martin's mother's family lived in Pennsylvania, and Martin's Uncle Kurt Weber was fighting for the North. Martin never talked about that.

When Nathan joined the other boys in the schoolyard, they were talking excitedly. Their words and ideas tumbled out like little streamlets rushing down a hillside after a storm. The Yankees will come to nearby Salem soon. They want to burn the railroad tracks. They'll steal the food and army supplies stored in Salem. Our army needs more soldiers. A recruiting patrol will soon be here to sign up more men.

"My pa will sign up," said one boy.

"Grandpa plans to join the Home Guard," another boy added. "Men in the Guard are mostly too old or too young to join the regular army. They're called to fight only when the war comes to their community."

"What about your pa?" Richard looked straight at Nathan.

"His pa's yeller," Martin answered before Nathan could speak. "He'll hide in the woods so the recruiters can't find him."

The other boys laughed.

That remark about Papa hurt Nathan, especially since it came from Martin. Martin and Nathan were close neighbors. For a long time they had been best friends. Lately things seemed to be different between them. That bothered Nathan. He thought the change began soon after Friedrick Speagle, Martin's father, left for the army.

The schoolmaster came to the door with a big bell in his hand. He rang the bell to call the children in. Nathan was glad to go inside.

All the children were in one room. They sat on wooden benches without backs. The smallest children were in the front of the room. The biggest ones were at the back.

Sometimes the older students helped the younger ones with their lessons. Nathan was always proud when the schoolmaster asked him to help someone.

But on this day, Nathan did not help anyone else. He had a hard time keeping his mind on his own studies. He even got one of his arithmetic problems wrong because he had not heard what the schoolmaster said.

When school was over for the day, Nathan left in a hurry. He didn't want to face the other boys. Nathan didn't think his papa was a coward. But it was true that he had refused to join the army. And Nathan had heard him talking to Mama about hiding if an army recruiter came back.

The first thing Nathan noticed when he got home was the huge stack of wood Papa had cut—enough to last for a long time.

Sure enough, Henry Garst was getting ready to leave. While he and Nathan fed the farm animals, he told his oldest son about his plans to hide in the mountains. Nathan was silent for a little while. Then he asked, "Papa, are you afraid to die?"

"I don't want to die and leave my family," his papa answered. "But I am not afraid of dying because I'll be with my Lord in heaven when I die. Why do you ask this question?"

Nathan hesitated. "The boys at school say you're yellow because you won't join the army."

"Is that what you think?" his father wanted to know.

"No, but I don't really understand why you and some of the other Brethren won't fight."

Henry leaned the pitchfork in the corner of the hayloft and sat down on a pile of hay. He motioned for Nathan to sit beside him. Henry looked at his son. "Do you know what baptism means?" Henry asked.

Nathan nodded. Uncle Abraham, mama's brother, and some other young men and women had been baptized last year. An elder had led his uncle out into a stream. He dipped him into the water three times. He laid his hand on his head and prayed. Then he led Uncle Abraham back to the river bank. The church members greeted him with a handshake and a kiss. "Baptism means joining the church," Nathan answered his papa's question.

"That's true," said Henry. "But it means a lot more, too. It means choosing another way of living—the way that Jesus taught. Do you know what I promised before I was baptized?"

Nathan shook his head.

"I promised to follow Jesus and to obey the Bible and the teachings of the church. Jesus is the Prince of Peace. He commands that we love everybody— even our enemies. He says that we must live in peace with all men and do no harm to any man. When I was baptized, I promised that I would never go to war. If I want to be a Christian and remain a member of our church, I cannot join the army. I must follow another way, the way of peace. Do you understand?"

"I think so," Nathan answered thoughtfully. "The reason you won't fight is not because you're afraid of being killed. It's because you cannot kill anybody else."

"Exactly. I couldn't have said it better myself." Henry patted his son's shoulder. Lately Nathan had sometimes thought that he was too big to be patted on his shoulder like a little child. But it felt good coming from Papa right now.

Nathan had another question. "Why are Uncle James and Uncle Elias fighting?"

Henry thought for a few moments before he spoke. "Your uncles are not members of the church yet, and they are not married. That means there's more pressure on them to join the army. And perhaps their understanding of Jesus' teachings is not the same as mine."

When they finished the chores and went inside, Nathan saw a blanket and some of Papa's warmest clothes on the bed. Ann Garst had gathered these things and some food supplies for her husband to take with him.

For supper that night they had Papa's favorite foods. They were Nathan's favorites, too. There were ham and gravy. There were potatoes and turnips from the root cellar. There were biscuits made with white flour and topped with butter and apple butter. There were even fried pies made from dried fruit.

After supper Papa got his Bible. He gathered his family around him. Tonight he read a story about Jesus and Peter. Some men wanted to kill Jesus. While Jesus was praying, his enemies came with swords and clubs to capture him. Peter pulled out his sword to defend Jesus. He even cut off the ear of one of Jesus' enemies. But Jesus told Peter to put away his sword. He healed the man's ear. Then Jesus went away quietly with those who had come to arrest him.

When Papa finished reading the story, the Garst family repeated the Twenty-third Psalm together: "The Lord is my shepherd; . . . I will fear no evil; for thou art with me" (Ps. 23:1a, 4b).

Henry prayed that God would help him follow Jesus and do what is right. He asked God to watch over and protect his family. He also prayed for the families of his friends, his neighbors, and even his enemies.

Henry hugged Nathan and Marshall and Monroe, holding each one close for a long time that night. Then Ann put Monroe in the cradle downstairs. She sent Nathan and Marshall upstairs to bed.

The next morning Nathan awoke early. When he went downstairs, Papa was gone.

CHAPTER 2

Yankees in the Valley

 On December 16, outriders brought word that Union Major General Averell was crossing Catawba Mountain into Roanoke County with a large army. The children at the Greenridge School were sent home.

When Nathan got home, Mama was carrying hams from the smokehouse. "We must hide enough food to last us through the winter and spring," Mama said. "The Yankees will steal what they can find."

They put the hams in sacks and hid them in the woodpile. They hid bags of flour, cornmeal, and dried beans under the straw mattresses on the beds. They took vegetables from the root cellar and buried them in a field.

All the families in the community hid food and anything of value. Fearfully they awaited the arrival of enemy troops.

Fortunately, the Union army did not enter the Greenridge area, but the Garsts and their neighbors could see a red glow and clouds of billowing smoke in the sky over the town of Salem just a few miles away.

In Salem the Union troops burned three depots that contained food and supplies waiting to be shipped to the Confederate army. They tore up railroad tracks, cut telegraph wires, and destroyed bridges and culverts.

When the Union army leaders learned of a Confederate plan to entrap them near Salem, the Yankees began to retreat almost as quickly as they had come. A line of Yankee soldiers stretched for four miles across the mountains.

That night the weather turned cold. Sleet and rain began to fall. Nathan helped Mama put big logs on the fire. Mama got extra comforts for the beds.

Nathan crawled into bed with his brother. He was exhausted from hard work and gnawing fear. But he could not sleep. His thoughts turned to Papa. Where was Papa tonight? Soldiers from both sides of the war had filled the woods and mountains. Had Papa been able to escape their eyes? If so, how would he protect himself from the cold and sleet?

Nathan heard Mama turn in her bed. He knew that she was worried, too.

Far up in the mountains Henry Garst was safe. That morning he had heard musket fire in the dis-

tance and had gone deeper into the woods, farther away from the sound of battle. He had watched the smoke billowing over Salem.

Sensing that a storm was coming, Henry found a small cave. Before the sleet began to fall, he cut some small pine branches and gathered some dry leaves. He took these into the cave. It was not safe to make a fire. That would alert his enemies to his presence.

Henry used the leaves and branches for a bed on the cold, damp floor of the cave. Drawing his coat around him, Henry lay down and covered himself with his blanket. He shivered, but it was not so much from the cold. His mind was not on the weather. His thoughts were on his wife and sons. He knew they had enough wood to keep them warm. But had soldiers destroyed or stolen their food? Were they safe from harm? Could he risk going back home to check on them? If he were captured and thrown into prison, who would care for them? Were his religious beliefs more important than his family? These thoughts sent shivers up his spine and kept sleep far from him.

By morning the sleet had stopped. The Yankees and the pursuing Rebels were on their way to Covington.

There was no school on this day. The schoolmaster and the boys were needed to help the army engineers and the old men in the area rebuild the bridges and culverts that had been destroyed north and east of Salem.

"Will Brethren help the army engineers rebuild?" Nathan asked his mama that morning.

"Yes," Ann replied. "Bridges and culverts help everyone in our community. Brethren will help in this work."

It was a day of hard work. Men and older boys cut logs and sawed lumber. Nathan and the younger boys carried rocks. The women and the girls cooked food and took it to the workers.

While they worked, Martin asked Nathan, "Where's your pa?" All the other boys looked at Nathan.

Nathan thought for awhile and said, "He's gone, but he is not afraid. He would risk his life to help another person but not to harm another."

"Oh yeah? Then why—" Richard was interrupted by the arrival of lunch brought by women who lived near where they were working.

There was little conversation during lunch. The hungry men and boys ate quickly so they could get back to work. There was no more talk about Henry Garst.

When night came, Nathan was so tired he could hardly eat supper. He crawled into bed and fell asleep.

Sometime during the night, Marshall shook Nathan. "Papa's home," Marshall whispered excitedly.

"No," Nathan said to his little brother. "You're dreaming. It's not safe for Papa to come home."

"But he IS here," Marshall insisted. "I heard him talking to Mama."

Nathan listened. Sure enough, Papa and Mama were talking softly in the darkness below.

Quietly the boys hurried downstairs and tumbled into Papa's arms.

Finally Nathan whispered, "Isn't it dangerous for you to be here?"

"I was very careful," Papa said. "I had to find out if my little family was safe. I think the soldiers and civilians are tired enough to sleep soundly tonight. They won't be out looking for me."

After the boys had gone back to bed, Papa left again, taking with him all the warm clothing, comforts, and food that he could carry.

Within four days the railroad tracks, the bridges, and the culverts had all been repaired. The last of the army engineers left Roanoke County.

Gradually things returned to normal in the valley. Still there was a lingering fear. The Yankees had come once. They might come again.

Henry stayed in hiding for several weeks. From time to time, he would come in the night to check on his family, to cut wood, and to see that they had the things they needed.

CHAPTER 3

A Neighbor's Loss

 It was Sunday. As usual, Nathan went with his mother and brothers to the Peters Creek meetinghouse. Many of the Brethren came on horseback, in buggies, or in wagons. Nathan's family lived less than a quarter of a mile away, and they always walked.

The meetinghouse was a plain brick building with clear glass windows and two doors. Two large fireplaces heated the building in winter. A loft above the main room provided sleeping space when visiting Brethren came for love feast.

Extending back from the main part of the building at one end was a kitchen where food was prepared for love feast.

Inside the large main room were plain wooden benches on each side of an aisle. At the front of the room were a long table and a long bench. Here the elders sat facing the church members.

The men went in the door at one end of the building and placed their broad-brimmed black hats on a wire rack above the aisle. The women with their children entered through the other door, placed their plain bonnets in another overhead rack, and sat down on the other side of the aisle.

When everyone was seated inside, a deacon started a hymn. Only a few people had hymnals. Most people had to repeat the words the deacon spoke. He read the first line aloud and then paused while everyone joined in singing that line. When they finished the line, he read the next line and waited again. He read each line of the hymn, pausing after each one so the people could sing. The hymn today was one of Nathan's favorites.

Guide me, O Thou great Jehovah,
Pilgrim through this barren land,
I am weak, but Thou art mighty,
Hold me with Thy powerful hand. . . .

Strong Deliverer,
Be Thou still my strength and shield.

Nathan had always liked this hymn because it reminded him of the stories of Moses in the Bible. Now it expressed his hope that God would take care of Papa and deliver him like he did the Hebrews in the wilderness.

When the hymn was finished, everyone turned to the back of the room and knelt for prayer, resting their elbows on the benches. One after another, several individuals prayed aloud with everyone joining in the Amen at the end of each prayer. Then prayer time was closed with the Lord's Prayer.

Prayer was followed by scripture reading. One of the elders read from Romans 12. The words "live peaceably with all men" (v. 18) caught Nathan's attention. There was also something about feeding your enemies and overcoming evil with good that he didn't fully understand yet.

Three different elders preached about the scripture. The sermons were almost always long. Usually Nathan began to wiggle and his mind started to wander during the preaching. But today he listened as the elders talked about the evils of war.

One elder told about John Naas, a Brethren man who lived in Germany many years before. He was a tall, strong man, and the king's men thought he would make a fine soldier in the king's army. But John Naas told them that Christ was his king. Even though they tortured him, he refused to serve in the army.

On this Sunday the elder at Peters Creek called upon Brethren men to stand firm in refusing to serve in the Confederate army, even in the face of threats, punishment, or imprisonment.

After the preaching, there were more prayers. Someone prayed for all the men of the church who were away from home trying to avoid the war. Nathan added his own silent prayer for his papa. He asked God to keep Papa safe from capture and torture.

There was another hymn, and then the service in the meetinghouse was over. But conversation about the service would continue in Brethren homes. On this Sunday, many Brethren from neighboring communities came to Peters Creek for worship. And every Peters Creek family would have visitors for dinner and fellowship afterward.

As he left the meetinghouse, Nathan wondered who would be coming to his home today. Usually he hoped there would be children near his own age. Today he wished that one of the visiting elders might come to his home. Sometimes these men had news about the war and its effect on Brethren.

It turned out that there were children in the crowd who gathered at the Garst home. And there was also a visiting elder from Botetourt County.

Ann Garst's kitchen was filled with the delicious smells of all kinds of food. But Nathan knew it would be a long time before he tasted food. The men would eat first, then the visiting women, and finally the children.

The weather was mild, and the older children played outside while waiting their turn to eat. They took turns rolling a barrel hoop with a piece of metal, and they played blindman's buff.

Then one of the boys suggested that they play the story of John Naas. Nathan wanted to be John, but his cousin Jacob got that role because he was the tallest boy in the group. Nathan had to be one of the king's soldiers. Nathan and another boy were trying to figure out how to torture John Naas when someone called them to dinner.

There was still plenty of food for the hungry boys and girls. While they were eating, Nathan could hear the men talking about the war. He ate quickly. Then he went over, sat on the floor near the men, and listened to their conversation.

Elder Moomaw was talking. He had been to Richmond where the Congress of the Confederacy was meeting: "The position of the Congress is clear. Brethren, Mennonites, Friends, and others who are opposed to war because of their religious convictions are exempted from military service if they pay the required tax. I think the government officials realize that it's useless to force men who will not fight into the army."

"Does that mean Papa and other Brethren men can come out of hiding and be safe?" Nathan asked. He knew that he should not interrupt his elders. Papa had told him many times that children should be seen and not heard when adults are talking. But Nathan just had to know the answer to his question.

Elder Moomaw wasn't angry. He looked at Nathan kindly. "No, son," he answered. "Unfortunately, there is still danger. Because of heavy battle losses, the army desperately needs more soldiers. Some of the recruiting officers refuse to recognize the religious exemption. We are having difficulty with the quartermaster in Roanoke County in this regard, too. He often refuses to allow Brethren the benefit of the exemption. Besides, there are always bushwhackers. These local soldiers often take it upon themselves to get rid of anyone they consider Union sympathizers."

Nathan shuddered at the words "get rid of." He knew that some Brethren and others had been imprisoned and some had been badly beaten. But Elder Moomaw's tone of voice made it clear that putting men in prison was not what bushwhackers had in mind when they thought of getting rid of someone.

Noting the fear in the young boy's eyes, Elder Moomaw laid his hand on Nathan's shoulder. "We usually know when soldiers or others who would harm your father are in the area," he said. "We pass along that word so that he will know when he should hide. He is a smart man and knows how to avoid danger."

One of the men in the room looked toward the window. The sun's position in the sky told him that it was time to start home. Milking and other farm chores had to be done on Sunday as well as on other days.

Soon all the visitors had gone. Ann and Nathan began their own evening chores.

※ ※ ※ ※ ※

March came. Willow trees began to show green, and plum trees were tinged with white. In the meadow a few venturesome dandelions and cowslips burst into bloom. The creeks ran full as the last of the winter snows melted. It was time to prepare fields for spring planting.

Fighting had not returned to the Roanoke Valley, and recruiters came less frequently. Henry Garst was no longer in hiding. Every day he worked with the old men, the boys, and some of the women plowing the fields. Henry volunteered to help his neighbors whose husbands and sons were away fighting. Some who had ridiculed his refusal to fight would not accept his offer of help. But most were glad for any assistance they could get.

Nathan's friend, Martin Speagle, didn't want Henry's help, but his mother, Greta, knew that she and Martin would not be able to prepare the ground and plant enough grain and vegetables to sustain their family. Martin's sisters were too small to help, and the Speagles had no relatives in Virginia. So reluctantly Martin worked side by side with his mother, Nathan, and Henry to plant spring crops.

One day when they were working in the Speagles' field, a horse and rider approached. It was a man from the Amsterdam post office. He handed Greta Speagle a letter.

Greta looked at the handwriting on the envelope. It was unfamiliar. Her face turned pale, and her hands shook. Sensing his mother's fear, Martin moved to her side. She continued to look at the unopened letter.

"Can I help?" Henry spoke gently.

Silently Greta handed the letter to him.

"Shall I read it?" he asked.

Greta nodded.

Henry read the letter. Friedrick Speagle and some other soldiers had been out foraging for food when they were surprised by Union soldiers. Friedrick had been shot and killed. He was buried in the graveyard of a small church in Culpeper County, not far from where the Confederate army was camped.

Henry looked at Nathan. "Go home and stay with your brothers. Tell your mama to come to the Speagles' house."

Henry and Martin led the shocked woman to her home. Greta did not speak. She stared straight ahead. Martin took his mama's hand. "I will take care of you," he told her bravely.

When Ann Garst arrived, she went to Greta and put her arms around her. The grieving woman began to sob softly.

Then Henry went to the neighboring Evans home to bring the three little Speagle girls home. Mrs. Evans came back with the girls.

Henry noticed Martin slip out of the house and head toward the barn. In a short time, Henry followed the boy. Martin sat on a pile of hay, his body and his face frozen in grief. Henry started to put a hand on the boy's shoulder, but Martin drew back.

Sensing Martin's feelings, Henry said, "It isn't fair that I'm here and your papa is not. Your papa was a good man. He loved you very much. You'll miss him more than anyone can know. I think your papa would want us to cry for him now so that we can be strong later for your mama and sisters."

At these words, Martin broke into tears, and so did Henry. Together the two cried—the boy for the father he would never see again, and the man for the fatherless child and the cruel and senseless war that had taken his neighbor's life.

Like all the neighbors, Ann Garst cooked food to take to the Speagles. Nathan watched his mama cook. "Mama," he said, "I want to show Martin that I care. But I don't know how to help him. And I'm not sure he wants my help."

Mama thought for a minute before she spoke. "You can go with me to take this food to the Speagles. Then you can tell Martin you're sorry about his papa."

"Will he believe me?" asked Nathan.

"I don't know." Mama was honest. "Why do you think he might not believe you? How would you feel if you were in his place?"

Nathan thought long and hard. "Maybe he's angry that his papa was killed and jealous that my papa is still here with us."

"You're probably right," Mama agreed. "It may take a while for him to believe you. All we can do right now is try to show him that we really do care."

Suddenly Nathan had an idea. "Do you remember the little flute Uncle Abraham carved for me?" he said. "Martin liked it. Would it be all right if I gave it to him?" Nathan asked his mama.

"Of course. It's a good way to show your sympathy," his mama replied.

Nathan knew that his papa wouldn't mind if he gave the flute away. When Uncle Abraham had given it to him, Papa had said that Brethren should not have any kind of musical instrument in their meetinghouses or homes. But Uncle Abraham had said, "I reckon if God didn't object to King David playing a harp, he wouldn't mind if Nathan has a small flute."

When Nathan and his mama arrived at the Speagles, other neighbors were there—mostly grownups. Martin was trying to keep his little sisters busy. Nathan went over to Martin. "I'm real sorry about your papa," he said. "I brought you

something." He pulled the flute from his pocket and handed it to Martin. Martin hesitated. Then, without a word, he reached out and took the flute.

Soon the farm families returned to their spring planting. Men and boys, women and girls worked from sunup to sundown.

Neighbors helped the Speagle family. Martin didn't talk a lot, but neither did he avoid Nathan when they were working in the fields. Often when workers stopped for water and a brief rest, Martin would go off alone. Sometimes Nathan saw him pull the wooden flute from his pocket and play a little tune. Nathan thought it was usually a sad tune. But it seemed to comfort the grieving boy.

CHAPTER 4

The Battle of Hanging Rock

 In June Henry Garst and a few other Brethren went into hiding again.

News drifted into the Greenridge community of renewed fighting in the Shenandoah Valley. It was said that the Union army would soon move out of the valley and seek to capture Lynchburg. A Union victory at Lynchburg would cut off the route that supplied food and provisions from southwestern Virginia to General Lee's army near Richmond.

Union General Hunter's attempt to capture Lynchburg failed. As the Brethren left their meeting-house on Sunday, June 19, a neighbor reported that outriders had brought news of the war. The Union army was retreating toward the Roanoke Valley. Hunter was a ruthless general who allowed his men to steal food, clothing, livestock, and anything of value. He ordered the burning of houses, farm buildings, and crops.

There were no leisurely Brethren gatherings for dinner and visiting that Sunday. Each family went to its own home. On Sundays the Brethren usually avoided work unless it was for feeding their families and caring for their animals. But on this Sunday everyone was busy trying to hide food and anything of value.

Ann Garst took the few coins saved for emergencies out of a big chest. She took a roll of rags she was saving to make rugs and unrolled the narrow strips of cloth. She placed the coins in a small bag and began to rewind the rags around the bag. Then she showed Marshall how to finish rewinding the rags into a ball.

Ann and Nathan decided to drive the livestock into the woods. If the invading soldiers did not find the animals, some would return home. Nathan would be able to find the others later and drive them back to the barn. Nathan went to the barn to carry out this plan.

Ann put most of the flour and cornmeal in bags and hid them. She left small amounts of each in the pantry. If soldiers raided the house, perhaps they would take what they found in the pantry and not search further. She did the same with the meat in the smokehouse, leaving a little there but hiding the rest.

That night Ann put Marshall and Monroe to bed in her room. Nathan, too, would spend the night there. Before the little boys went to sleep, Ann asked Nathan to read from the Bible. He read from Psalm 46:

God is our refuge and strength
a very present help in trouble.
Therefore we will not fear.

Then Mama prayed: "Dear God, please protect us. Stay with Papa wherever he is tonight, and watch over our neighbors, too. As Jesus taught us, we also pray for our enemies and ask for peace to come to our land. Amen."

Ann blew out the candles. In the dark silence, Nathan wondered where Papa was and if he knew the Yankees were nearby. Nathan was not sure that he could truthfully say he did not fear, like the scripture said. Many others were fearful, too. There was little sleep in the Garst home, the Greenridge community, or the Roanoke Valley that night.

On Monday a quiet watchfulness hung over the Greenridge community. People tried to go about their daily chores. The cows that Nathan had driven into the woods came back to the barn. Nathan and Ann milked them. Then Nathan chased them back into the woods. No soldiers were seen that day. An uneasy darkness settled over the community.

During the night a restless Nathan looked out the window. In the southeast toward Big Lick, the glow of fires lit the night sky. Ann joined Nathan at the window. Both of them knew that the Yankees were within a few miles of their home.

"I wonder where Papa is," Nathan worried. "Do you think he can see the fires? Will he be safe?"

"The Yankees will probably move west toward Salem instead of coming our way. If Papa is anywhere near here, he will see the fires and move farther into the mountains," Ann tried to reassure her son.

Later during the night, they saw fires in the direction of Salem. There was no sleep that night for Nathan or his mama.

Before long Nathan heard a horse whinny in the night. "Listen, Mama," he whispered. Straining their ears, they could hear the movement of horses.

"I will fear no evil," Mama said. But Nathan thought her voice trembled a little. He was glad his little brothers were sleeping soundly and peacefully.

For what seemed like hours, Ann and Nathan waited and listened. A cavalry unit was passing up Cove Road, which skirted the Garst farm not more than four hundred yards from the house. Finally the muffled sound of the moving horses faded in the distance. Nathan and Ann breathed a sigh of relief. "They must have been Confederate soldiers," Nathan said. He was right.

When daylight came, all was quiet near the Garst farm. No soldiers could be seen anywhere. But at the edge of the farm, hoofprints on the dusty ground gave proof that a large group of horses had passed that way during the night.

About midmorning the Garst family heard artillery fire to the north. A Brethren deacon who came by to see if the family was all right reported fighting at Hanging Rock. There, at a gap in the mountains, the road from Salem and Cove Road met at the New Castle Pike, which led over Catawba Mountain toward West Virginia.

Union forces, pursued by Confederate troops, were fleeing from Salem toward West Virginia. The Southern cavalry unit that the Garsts had heard during the night attacked the Yankees at the gap. Throughout the morning and into the afternoon, Nathan heard the sounds of battle. He could see and smell smoke from the fighting. One thought kept going through his mind. Where is Papa? If the huge army of soldiers going over the mountain spilled over from the road into the forests, would Papa be in danger?

By the end of the day, the battle of Hanging Rock was over. Some of the wounded soldiers were brought to the Brethren meetinghouse to be cared for. Nathan watched his little brothers while his mama took food to the meetinghouse for the wounded men.

The Brethren women who did not have young children at home and the older men stayed at the

meetinghouse to care for the wounded soldiers—
some from the Confederate army and some from the
Union army, abandoned in the hasty retreat.

When Ann came home from the meetinghouse,
Marshall asked if any Yankee soldiers were there.

"Yes," his mother answered.

Nathan was thoughtful. Then he asked, "Mama,
if Brethren don't believe in war, why do we take
care of soldiers who will fight again when they get
well?"

"We don't want them to fight again," said Ann,
"but we believe that followers of Christ should help
to heal anyone who is injured, whether they be
friends or foes. Do you remember how Jesus healed
the ear of the man who was going to deliver him to
be crucified?"

Nathan remembered the story well.

※ ※ ※ ※ ※

From his hiding place on the mountainside,
Henry Garst had seen the battle of Hanging Rock.
His heart ached at the cruel sight of fellow country-
men killing one another. What could he do to stop
the fighting? he wondered.

Before the day was over, Henry watched the
Union army retreat up Catawba Mountain. He saw
most of the Southern forces withdraw in the opposite
direction. He saw men removing the wounded from

the battlefield. He knew they would take the injured to homes and churches to be cared for. He longed to help the wounded, but he knew that his own life would be in grave danger if he tried to do so.

When night came, all was quiet on the mountain. Henry was kneeling on a large rock praying for his family, his friends, and his enemies. Suddenly he thought he heard a weak cry. He listened carefully. The sound came again—the low moan of someone in pain. Henry rose and moved in the direction of the sound.

He came upon a man lying in some bushes. The wounded soldier had been shot in battle. He managed to tell Henry that he stayed on his runaway horse until he was thrown in this place. Before he could say more, the soldier lost consciousness. Henry felt the man's pulse. His heart was still beating.

Henry could not see well enough in the dark to examine the man carefully. Lighting a torch would be dangerous. Still he must help his brother. He cut a dead branch from a tree, lit it, and stuck the other end in the ground.

He saw that the soldier's wounded leg was bleeding badly. Henry tore a piece from his own shirt and made a tourniquet to stop the bleeding. He knew that he must get the soldier to a place where a doctor could help him. Carefully he put out the torch. He lifted the man to his shoulders and started down the mountain.

Hours later, Henry arrived at the Brethren meetinghouse. A doctor and many others were caring for the wounded in the loft of the meetinghouse. Staying in the shadows, Henry laid the man in the blue uniform inside the meetinghouse. Then he stepped out into the thick darkness.

Outside, he felt a hand on his shoulder. Henry stiffened. "Shh–," a voice whispered. It was Elder Brubaker, who had recognized Henry. In a very soft voice, he told Henry that his family was safe and well. He warned Henry that he should leave as quickly as possible and get back to the forest before dawn. He dare not risk stopping at home even though it was so very close.

Henry ached to see his wife and children. But he knew that if he were captured, he might never see them again. Warily, he made his way back to a safe hiding place.

CHAPTER 5

Yankee Spy or Loving Uncle?

Early the next day, there was a knock on the door of the Garst home. Ann was surprised to see Elder Brubaker. She invited him inside.

Marshall and Monroe were still asleep. Nathan, who was getting ready to go to the barn, waited inside to see what brought Elder Brubaker to their home so early.

After the elder greeted the Garsts, he said, "I was at the meetinghouse all night helping to care for the wounded. I saw Henry a few hours ago."

Before Elder Brubaker could continue, Nathan blurted out, "Was papa wounded?"

"No, son," the elder replied. "Your papa is fine. He did a very brave deed. He found a badly injured Union soldier in the woods and brought him to the meetinghouse."

"Who saw him?" Ann asked anxiously. She knew that Confederate soldiers and even some of their neighbors would be all too eager to turn Henry over to army recruiters, especially if they knew that he had saved a Yankee's life.

"I feel sure that I'm the only one who saw him," the elder continued. "And I sent him away at once. I was afraid he would stop to see you. I warned him that would be extremely dangerous at this time. I told him you were all fine and promised to let you know that he is well. He should be in the thick woods of the mountain now. "

Ann and Nathan breathed sighs of relief.

"I don't think you should tell anyone at all that Henry was here," the elder warned. "We never know who might let such information slip. And in the hands of the wrong person, it could be disastrous."

Ann and Nathan assured Elder Brubaker they wouldn't tell anyone about Henry's deed. Ann thanked the elder for letting them know that Henry was safe and well.

All day long Nathan thought about his papa. He thought about him while he fed the animals and milked the cows. He thought about him while he suckered the young corn. Elder Brubaker could be sure that the secret about what Papa had done was perfectly safe with Nathan. Why, it almost seemed that Papa cared more about the enemy soldier than his own family, risking his life that way.

Nathan yanked a little shoot from a stalk of corn a bit too vigorously and pulled the good stalk from the ground.

Why did Papa try to save the Yankee? Wasn't it a foolish thing to do?

In his mind, Nathan could hear his papa's answer to those questions. "Jesus told us to love our enemies. He said we should feed them if they are hungry. Surely he would also say we should help them if they are injured."

Well, maybe Papa could do that. But Nathan was not sure that he would try to save his enemy when it meant risking his own life.

Later that day, Ann asked Nathan to take some cornbread to the meetinghouse. She had baked it for the wounded soldiers there.

There were very few men from the community at the meetinghouse. Nathan learned from one of the women that the men were still at Hanging Rock, where they had worked all day long to bury the soldiers and horses killed in the battle.

When Nathan took the cornbread to the kitchen, one of the women asked him to carry a jug of water to the loft. He was surprised to see Greta Speagle and Martin in the loft. Greta was putting a wet towel on the forehead of a wounded man who lay on a bed of straw. Martin was standing nearby, looking very uncomfortable. In fact, when he saw Nathan, Martin looked like he wanted to disappear. He quickly turned away without speaking to Nathan.

While Nathan was wondering how he should react, Greta Speagle noticed him. She motioned for him to come nearer.

"This is my brother, Kurt Weber," she said. She nodded toward the wounded man. "He was injured in the battle. Someone found him and brought him here. The doctor had to remove one of his legs. He's still unconscious."

While she was speaking, Nathan noticed the blue jacket folded neatly beside the unconscious soldier. He remembered that Martin's uncle was in the Union army. Papa had told Nathan that. Martin had never talked about it. That explained why Martin was so troubled now.

"I'm sorry about your brother," Nathan spoke directly to Greta Speagle. "I hope he will be better soon."

Recognizing Martin's feelings, Nathan changed the subject. "Grandpa helped me make a new kind of rabbit trap," he told Martin. "Would you like to go with me to check it? It's not far from here. Maybe there will be a rabbit for stew."

"Go along if you wish," Martin's mama said. "But be back here before the sun reaches the top of Fort Lewis Mountain."

As they walked along, Nathan described the trap and explained how it worked. "It's a long box with a door at one end. At the other end, a stick goes down through a hole into the box. Behind the stick is food to attract the rabbit. On the other end of the stick is a string tied to the raised door. When the rabbit hits the stick inside the trap, the string releases the door. It slides down and traps the rabbit inside."

When the boys drew near the trap, Nathan said excitedly, "Look, the door is down. There's a rabbit inside."

Just then the boys heard a scratching sound inside the trap. A loud MEOW followed.

"That's a strange-sounding rabbit," laughed Martin. Nathan opened the door a little bit and peered inside. There was a neighbor's large cat. He raised the door all the way, and the angry cat rushed out.

"I guess we won't have rabbit stew tomorrow," Nathan admitted. "But at least we know the trap works."

Martin was fascinated by the trap. "I think I could help you make a trap like this one," Nathan offered, "if we can find some wooden planks."

As the boys parted, they promised to keep their eyes open for suitable wood.

❈ ❈ ❈ ❈ ❈

Before long the wounded soldiers all left the meetinghouse. A few of the Confederate soldiers were transferred to army hospitals. Others would never be able to fight again and were sent home.

Most of the Union soldiers were sent to a camp for prisoners of war.

Kurt Weber had shown some improvement. He asked for permission to stay with his widowed sister and her family. Perhaps, if he got stronger, he could be of some help to Greta and her children.

After many letters and conferences with officials, his request was granted, but only after a soldier in the Home Guard agreed to see that he would not try to escape or have any contact with the enemy.

A summer of hard work lay ahead for everyone in the Roanoke Valley. Again bridges and culverts had been destroyed. Railroads had been severely damaged. Houses, barns, and factories on the southeast side of the valley and in Salem had been burned by General Hunter's army. Some crops had been destroyed and had to be replanted. The old men, the women, and the children set to work to repair the damage as best they could.

At harvest time, everyone worked together first on one farm and then another to save the precious grain. In early July, neighbors worked on the Evans farm. Nathan and Martin were helping. So were many of their classmates from school.

Men who were too old to fight in the war and some women cut the golden grain with large scythes. Boys and girls gathered the stalks into bundles and tied them together. Others stacked the sheaves, or bundles of wheat, in shocks. There the wheat would stay until the grain was threshed, or separated from the straw.

Nathan was working near Martin when one of the girls from school called to Martin, "Are you really hiding a Yankee spy in your house?" Several boys and girls laughed.

Martin's face turned a brilliant red with shame. But it was Nathan who spoke. "Kurt Weber is not a spy. He's a wounded man who loves his sister and her children and wants to help them. And he is not hiding."

Nathan turned to Martin. "Come on," he said. "Let's go get a drink of water."

The boys walked in silence over to a tree that was shading several big pails of water. Each drank a big dipper of the cool water. "It sure would be good to sit in the shade for a while," Nathan said, "but I reckon we have to get back to work."

The boys wiped the sweat from their foreheads and went back to their tasks. This time they worked in a different part of the field with Nathan's grandpa, mama, and some other Brethren. Nathan knew none of them would tease Martin.

When the sun was directly overhead, the workers stopped harvesting. At a small stream, they dipped water with their hands and splashed their hot, dusty faces. Then everyone gathered around a huge table in the Evans's yard. The table was filled with food prepared by Nannie Evans and older neighbor women who were not working in the field.

When Nathan had filled his plate with food, his eyes searched the yard for Martin, but Martin was nowhere to be seen. After a short rest, workers returned to the field. It was then that Nathan saw Martin join a group of harvesters. Nathan guessed that Martin had gone off by himself to eat his dinner. He supposed Martin had a lot to think about.

When the day's work was over, Martin joined the Garst family and rode home with them in their wagon.

There was not much conversation on the way home. Everyone was too tired to do much talking. But when they got off the wagon at the Garst house, Martin said to Nathan, "Uncle Kurt is a great comfort to Mama. I know he's not a spy, but most everyone thinks he is. I'm beginning to understand how you feel when some of us call your pa a coward."

Martin turned and hurried home. As Nathan went toward his own house, he wondered when the terrible war would end. And when it did end, would people who had disagreed ever be friends again? He wished he could talk to Papa about that.

※ ※ ※ ※ ※

The summer of hard work dragged on. Fighting did not return to the Roanoke Valley, but there was heavy fighting in Georgia and in northern Virginia. It even reached the outskirts of Washington, D. C.

Earlier in the year, the Confederate Congress had extended the ages of the draft to include all able-bodied men between the ages of 17 and 50. Roanoke County had mustered a unit of men ages 16 to 18 and 55 to 60. People referred to these men as the Cradle to Grave Unit. Most men in between were already in the army. Even some of the older boys at Nathan's school had gone to war.

Brethren families in Virginia faced renewed scorn and hatred for their refusal to join the army. In June, John Kline, a beloved Brethren preacher and leader, was ambushed and murdered by Confederate irregulars in Rockingham County. Brother Kline had been moderator of the Annual Meeting of the Brethren for four years. The moderator is the highest position in the church. Just before his death, he led the discussions in Indiana at the Annual Meeting. At that meeting, Brethren were urged to endure whatever sufferings might come and to make whatever sacrifices necessary to maintain their principles of peace and nonviolence.

At the same time, some Brethren men left Virginia and fled to northern states. Others, including Henry Garst, continued to hide.

Once in a long time when it was very dark, Henry would carefully make his way home and check on his family. But most of the time he remained in hiding. It was too dangerous to leave his mountain hideaway.

CHAPTER 6

A Dangerous Mission

 One fall day when Nathan was coming home with a string of fish he had caught, he saw a strange horse tied to the fence near the house. Who was here? Fear crept over him. Was it a Confederate scout looking for Papa? Would Mama be able to convince him that she didn't know where Papa was?

Nathan crept to the window and looked in. The visitor was Elder Moomaw. Nathan didn't know why he was here, but he was sure his mission was a friendly one. The boy breathed easier.

When Nathan entered the door, Elder Moomaw was already standing to leave. He greeted Nathan warmly. Before taking his leave, he complimented the boy on his fine catch of fish.

The relief Nathan felt was short-lived. Mama's face was clouded with anxiety, and the piece of paper she was holding trembled in her hand.

"What's the matter, Mama?" Nathan asked. Mama glanced at the windows and door to be sure no one was listening. Then she shared the news that Brother Moomaw had brought.

Brethren men in the Shenandoah Valley had been imprisoned for refusing to serve in the Confederate army. Others had been beaten and threatened. General Sheridan, who was leading the invading army in the Shenandoah Valley, had offered teams, wagons, and military protection to transport Brethren and other peace-loving people through the Confederate lines into the North. The refugees would depart from Harrisonburg.

The paper in Mama's hand contained the names and addresses of people who would help Brethren reach Harrisonburg if they wanted to cross the lines of fighting and leave Virginia.

"Your grandpa is away helping with the harvest. There is no one to warn your papa of the increasing danger and to give him this information," said Mama.

"I know where Grandpa leaves messages for Papa," Nathan said. "He showed me the place once when we were looking for huckleberries. He told me about the signal he uses to contact Papa, too. I am not sure I can find the place at night, but I will try."

"You are a brave boy," Mama said. "But I can't let you go into the mountains alone at night."

"Then let me go early tomorrow morning. I'll take a basket and pick chinquapins. No one will suspect me of carrying a message. I'll stay overnight with Papa if I find him there. If I don't see him, I'll stay alone in the cave where he hides. Then I'll leave the message and food for him and come home."

Nathan shivered at the possibility of staying alone on the mountain at night. But he was careful not to let his mama see his fear.

Since there seemed to be no other way, Mama reluctantly agreed to Nathan's plan. With straw she wove a false bottom for an old basket. Next she wrote a letter to Papa and hid it with the message from Elder Moomaw and some blank pages between the old and the new bottoms of the basket. Then she carefully wove the two bottoms together. In the basket she put some bread, meat, and dried fruit. "Eat a little of this food if you get hungry, but save most of it for Papa," she told her son. "There's little food to be found in the mountains at this time of year, except nuts and maybe persimmons."

Nathan slept very little that night. He rose before the sun was up. "Now remember," Mama said, "if anyone sees you, tell them you're hunting chinquapins and you brought a little lunch with you. Watch carefully to be sure no one is following you."

Ann hugged Nathan and then watched him until he disappeared into the dark woods at the edge of the farm.

At first there was a little clearing in the woods where Papa had cut wood and dragged it out of the forest. Nathan moved quickly along through the clearing. Before long, all traces of a path disappeared. The trees were thick and the underbrush dense. He made his way carefully up the first ridge.

Several small ridges, each a little higher than the one before it, lay between him and the mountain where Papa hid. Briars tore at Nathan's clothes as he pushed through thickets. A sudden rattle reminded him to watch out for snakes. Whenever he found chinquapins or nuts of any kind, he put them in the basket, covering the food he carried.

When the sun was almost overhead, he stopped by a stream for a drink. Using two rocks, he cracked and ate a few nuts, saving the precious bread, meat, and fruit for Papa.

By late afternoon, he was in a grove of oak and hickory trees. Looking around, he saw a tree whose yellow-green leaves had white woolly undersides. It was the chinquapin tree near Papa's hideout. Most of the chinquapins in the forest grew on bushes, but this was a big tree. Nathan's eyes searched the woods in every direction. He listened for any human sound. He found no sign that anyone had been in this area.

Nathan began to pick up chinquapins. As he did so, he gave the call of a bobwhite. Then he listened attentively. From somewhere in the distance, the call came back. It was not the call Nathan was expecting. It might be the call of a real bobwhite or of someone who had guessed that it was a signal. Nathan waited longer. Then the sweet mournful call of a pewee penetrated the forest. Nathan's heart skipped a beat. That was Papa's signal. Nathan returned the call to indicate that all was clear.

Nathan continued to gather nuts. After a while, without a sound, Papa appeared. Henry hugged his son and held him close for a long moment. Then he held him at arm's length and looked at him fondly. "What a sight for sore eyes!" Papa laughed.

Papa assured Nathan that he had seen no bush-whackers or patrols for days. He led Nathan to the well-hidden cave that was his hideout. Once inside, Papa was full of questions. How are Mama and your little brothers? Where is Grandpa? How are the crops and garden? What is the spirit of the Brethren meeting?

Nathan answered the questions as well as he could.

Then the boy remembered the basket. Pouring the nuts on the floor of the cave, he gave Papa the food he had brought and told him about the hidden letter. Papa laid aside the welcomed food and eagerly took out the letter. Tears filled his eyes as he read his wife's loving words.

Papa was disturbed by Elder Moomaw's news about increased pressure on those who refused military service. He told Nathan that if possible he would like to come home at night and talk with mama about what he should do, but since that might prove too dangerous, he wrote her a letter on the blank sheets of paper that came with her letter. Papa put the letter in the basket, carefully replaced the false bottom, and secured it with dry twigs from a wild grapevine. Then he helped Nathan put the nuts he had gathered back into the basket. They went outside and added more chinquapins until the basket was almost full.

Only then did Papa enjoy a little of the food that Mama had sent. Nathan refused to eat the precious food he had brought from home. He satisfied his hunger with nuts.

When night fell, Nathan snuggled against his papa. They talked until late in the night. At last Nathan fell asleep.

Before dawn the next day, Nathan ate more nuts and one small piece of dried fruit. Sadly he hugged his papa, said good-bye, and set out for home. Before he was out of sight, he turned and looked at his papa for a long time.

During the morning, Nathan saw no signs that humans had been in the area. Then, without warning, a shot rang out. Quickly Nathan hid behind a huge tree, his heart pounding. After a short time, he peered around the tree trunk. A few yards away, a Confederate soldier was picking up a rabbit he had shot. At that moment the soldier saw Nathan.

"Come out from behind that tree, boy," the ragged soldier commanded. He dropped the rabbit and pointed his gun at Nathan.

Nathan stepped forward, trying to hide his fear.

"What're you doing here?" the soldier demanded.

"Looking for chinquapins," Nathan answered as calmly as he could.

"Bring me them nuts," the soldier snarled.

Nathan's mind flashed to the letter hidden in the basket. He pushed back his panic and thought quickly.

"Yes, sir," he replied and started forward. Then suddenly he tripped, dropping the basket and scattering the nuts.

"You clumsy brat," the man scowled. He kicked Nathan. Then, relishing meat more than the scattered nuts, he picked up his rabbit and strode off down the ridge.

Nathan lay there trembling with terror, pain, and relief. Slowly he got up. He decided to retrieve as many of the nuts as possible in case he should meet anyone else who wanted to know what he was doing in the woods.

Still shaking from what could have been a disastrous encounter, Nathan hurried toward home. Finally, as he neared the slopes of the last ridge, he heard voices! This time he hid quickly and did not peek out. He listened carefully. One voice was that of the soldier he had met earlier. The other voice was Martin's.

"I'm looking for deserters or Union sympathizers. You seen anybody on the mountain?" the soldier asked.

Did Martin see me leave yesterday? Nathan wondered. If he knows I've been gone overnight, he will guess why. Will he tell the soldier? Nathan held his breath.

"I didn't see nobody but another boy gathering nuts," Martin answered the soldier.

The voices moved off in the distance. Nathan lay still for a long time. He had had two close escapes. He decided to wait until nightfall to continue his journey. Mama would be worried, but he could not risk losing Papa's letter to a soldier.

Back at the farm, Ann Garst watched and waited and prayed. When midafternoon came and Nathan was not back, she grew anxious. Was Nathan lost? Had he been hurt? Had an enemy followed him to his papa's hiding place? Had Nathan and Henry both been captured?

Ann forced herself to work, but every few minutes she went to the window and looked out toward the woods.

When she had milked the cows and fed the animals, she fixed supper for Marshall and Monroe. She was too worried to eat anything.

At dusk Ann lit a candle and placed it in the window. She put the little boys to bed. She took her Bible and began to read from Isaiah:

*Fear thou not; for I am with thee;
be not dismayed; for I am thy God;
I will strengthen thee;
yea, I will help thee.*

Ann was praying that God would be with her husband and her son when there was a sound at the door. It was Nathan, tired and hungry, but safe!

While he ate, Nathan told his mama all that had happened. Then he fell asleep from exhaustion.

Ann spent most of the night reading and rereading her husband's letter. She thanked God for protecting her family. She prayed that he would continue to keep them safe and guide them in deciding what to do.

❄ ❄ ❄ ❄ ❄

At his hiding place on the mountain, Henry read and reread his wife's letter. He studied Elder Moomaw's notes about escaping to the North.

What should he do? He dared not go home. So many people hated the Brethren who refused to fight. So many were eager to capture or kill him. With winter coming, there would be little food available in the woods. And it was becoming increasingly dangerous for anyone to bring him food.

His God and his church had told him that he must not go to war and that he must suffer in order to be true to Jesus, the Prince of Peace.

It seemed that the only thing to do now was to leave his home and family. He must try to join the Brethren in Harrisonburg and cross the lines of battle. Ann had said that she and the boys would pray for him and await his return to them.

If only he could talk to Ann about this decision. If only he could say good-bye to her and the children. But he decided that any attempt to return home now would not only be risking his own life but might also endanger his family.

Tearing a page from his Bible, Henry underlined a verse and made some marks. Then he wrote in the margin *Hymn No. 201.* He dared not write more or sign his name or give the date. He put the page in the hollowed-out place under the chinquapin tree where he had received and left messages. Carefully he covered the spot with dirt and dry leaves.

Every night Ann wondered if Henry might try to come home. And when he did not come, she wondered where he was and if he was safe.

Then one day in late September, Grandpa Garst stopped to see Ann and the boys. He told them that he had been to the mountain hideaway. There was no response to his signal call and no sign of Henry. It was impossible to tell that anyone had lived in the cave.

But in the secret message place, he had found a page from the Bible.

Ann and Nathan recognized Henry's handwriting in the margin. Ann read aloud the verse that Henry had underlined: "The Lord watch between me and thee, when we are absent one from another" (Gen. 31:49). Then she got her hymnal and looked at Hymn No. 201. It was a hymn about parting.

Ann and Nathan knew that Papa left in hopes of reaching safety in the North. They knew that it would be a long time before they saw Papa again. The little boys did not understand their mama's sadness, but they seemed to sense it.

Nathan looked again at the page in his mama's hand. He reread the underlined verse—Papa's prayer for them. Then he noticed small marks under two other words near the beginning of the page. The first word was *And*; the second one was *with*.

"Why are those words marked?" Nathan wondered aloud. "Do they mean something?"

"No, son," Ann replied. "Papa probably marked them accidentally when he was reading with a pen in his hand."

Nathan took the page and looked at it for a long time. Then he spoke. "I think I know when Papa left. I think he left September 25."

"What makes you think that?" Grandpa asked.

"I think Papa meant to mark those words. The word *And* is the ninth word on the page. *September* is the ninth month in the year. The word *with* is the twenty-fifth word on the page. That would be the day he left."

"You may be right," his mama said thoughtfully. "That would be the second day after you took my letter and Elder Moomaw's message to him."

Days stretched into weeks, and there was no word from Papa. Had he reached Harrisonburg safely? Had safe passage through the battle lines been provided for Brethren and other peace-loving people as promised by General Sheridan?

Ann Garst and her sons could only trust that God was watching over Papa while he was absent from them. Every night they prayed for strength to carry on without him.

In late October, Elder Moomaw from the Valley meetinghouse in Botetourt County brought news to the Peters Creek meetinghouse. Many wagons filled with Brethren and others left Harrisonburg under military protection. They had been taken to Martinsburg, West Virginia. From there many of them took trains west. It was good news for many families in Virginia; still the elder did not know whether Henry Garst or other Brethren from the Roanoke Valley were among the group that left.

CHAPTER 7

Hoping for a Letter

Weeks passed and still there was no news from Henry. Nathan thought about his papa as he and Mama worked to get ready for another winter without him. They stored potatoes and turnips in the root cellar. They dried apples. They shucked and shelled corn. They took some of the corn to the mill and had it ground into hominy and cornmeal. With Grandpa's help, they butchered hogs. They made the fat into lard and salted the meat to preserve it through the winter.

One day Grandpa brought news of Uncle James and Uncle Elias. It was not good news. Both men had been captured in the fighting at Winchester. They were in a Union prisoner of war camp. Their letter was short. Parts of it had been blotted out.

"They probably weren't allowed to write about the battle or conditions in the camp," Grandpa said.

"We don't even know if they were injured. But at least we know they're not in the middle of the fighting now. That's one thing to be thankful for."

Fall turned into winter. Still there was no news from Henry. It was hard not knowing if he was safe and where he might be. Every night Ann and the boys read the Bible and prayed for Papa.

One night Nathan said, "I wish we had a picture of Papa. It would help us remember him. Martin has a picture of his papa."

"Annual Meeting has said that Brethren should not have their pictures made," Mama explained. "The Ten Commandments say we should not make images. Besides, we don't need a picture to remind us of Papa. He is in our minds and hearts."

That night before he went to sleep, Nathan tried to picture Papa in his mind. He could see his dark hair and beard. He could see his bright brown eyes that twinkled when he laughed and blazed when he spoke sternly. Still it would be nice to have a picture of him, Nathan thought. It would be a picture with eyes twinkling like Papa's did when he was pleased with something you had done.

Winter came, and 1864 turned into 1865. Still there was no news from or about Henry Garst.

Then, one day in January, a letter came. Ann and Nathan recognized the handwriting at once. Papa had written a letter. He must be safe. Ann gathered the family around her and read the letter aloud.

Papa was in Virden, Illinois, and he was reasonably well. He wrote about how difficult it had been to leave his family without a chance to say good-bye. He told how much he missed his wife and boys. He wrote about the dangerous and difficult trip to Illinois. He told how he again and again thanked the kind and merciful God who protected him from all danger and helped him to do no harm to any man.

The letter ended with a prayer that God would be with his little family through all the trials and troubles of this life and that God would help all of them to do his will.

It was a happy day for the Garst family. Nathan rode over to share the good news with Grandma and Grandpa Garst. Ann asked a neighbor to ride to the home of her mama and tell her about the letter.

That night Ann read Papa's letter to the children again. Their prayers were filled with thankfulness to God for watching over Papa and keeping him safe while he was away from them.

Marshall, who was not quite four, said, "Thank you, God, for Papa's letter." And even Monroe, who could not understand what had happened, smiled happily. He sensed the feelings of his mama and brothers.

That night as Nathan lay in bed, the moon shone brightly through the window and made a little path across the floor. That same moon is shining on Papa in Illinois, Nathan thought. I can see him now, reading his Bible in the moonlight. I can see him kneeling in prayer. I can hear him praying for us.

Nathan felt very close to Papa. Mama is right, he thought. I can see Papa in my mind, and I can feel him in my heart. Maybe I don't need an image of him on paper.

The next day Ann and Nathan both wrote long letters to Papa. They were happy letters filled with news about their daily lives, the farm, the other family members, and the church. But most of all, they were filled with joy because Henry was safe.

Ann and the boys still missed Henry very much. But knowing that he was well and among friends eased the loss they felt.

❖ ❖ ❖ ❖ ❖

One Saturday in early March, Grandpa brought Grandma over to visit while he went to the mill to have some corn ground into cornmeal.

The weather was mild, and Ann needed soap. Grandma volunteered to watch Marshall and Monroe while Ann and Nathan made soap. Ann asked Nathan to start the fire.

Nathan got some kindling and several logs from the woodpile. He piled them in the center of a large metal ring that stood on four metal legs. He helped his mama set a big iron kettle into the ring. Then he started the fire under the kettle.

All winter Ann had been saving grease when she cooked meat. She poured this grease into the kettle. Nathan stirred the grease while she added some water. Then she got some pails in which wood ashes had been soaking in water to make lye. She poured the liquid off the ashes carefully so that the ashes would stay on the bottom of the pail.

Ann added the lye to the kettle. While the soap boiled, she and Nathan took turns stirring it.

"It's sure been a long time since Papa's letter came," Nathan said as he stirred the bubbling liquid. "I wonder if he's all right. Do you think he got the letters we wrote to him?"

"I hope so," Ann replied, "but the mail is very slow these days. And sometimes it doesn't get through at all, especially when it has to cross the battle lines. It would be good to hear from Papa. But at least we know he's in a safe place now."

"I sure miss Papa," Nathan said.

"So do I," said Ann. "And I'm sure he misses us. You and your brothers and I have each other and your grandmas and grandpa. Papa is separated from all of his family. I'm certainly thankful for the good Brethren in Illinois who have taken him in."

When the soap had boiled long enough, they poured it into long flat pans. Later, when it was cold and hard, Ann would cut it into bars.

Nathan put out the fire and washed the kettle while his mama took the leftover ashes and dumped them on the garden. They would make the soil rich.

Grandma had cooked a good dinner. While they ate, she told the boys stories about her life as a young girl.

When dinner was over, Mama told Nathan he could read until time to do the evening chores.

Nathan was pleased. There was so little time for reading. He went upstairs and picked up a book that a classmate had loaned him. The book was called *Robinson Crusoe*. This story about a man who was shipwrecked on a desert island was quite different from Papa's books that Nathan sometimes read. He found the adventure very exciting. He was so engrossed in the story that he did not hear Grandpa when he came to get Grandma.

Marshall came upstairs. "Grandpa's here. Come downstairs," he said.

Grandpa smiled at the boys. "I brought you a very special surprise," he told them. Guess what it is."

"New shoes?" guessed Marshall. He looked at his shoes that were worn and pinched his toes.

"Shoe," echoed Monroe. He was just learning to talk and repeated whatever his brother said.

Grandpa looked at Nathan and waited for him to guess.

"A letter from Papa?" Nathan asked excitedly. That was the surprise that would please him most. And he knew that Grandpa always stopped at the post office when he was near it.

"Nathan is right," Grandpa said. He pulled out a letter and handed it to Ann.

"Maybe we can get new shoes for you next fall." He patted the little boys on their heads. "It won't be long now until the weather is warm enough for you to go barefooted."

Mama read Papa's letter aloud.

Virden, 1865 February the 23
Macoupin County, Illinois

Dear and Most Affectionate Companion,
I take my pen in hand this evening to drop you a few lines to let you hear from me once more. I am in moderate health at this time and I truly hope and trust to the Lord that these few lines may reach you and find you all well. Jeremiah has got nearly well again. He is at work again though he is not very stout yet. There is a great deal of sickness in this country.

Well, Ann, I have not received no letter from you yet. And I want to hear from you all very bad.

Ann, I long to see you and Nathan and Marshall and Monroe. Poor little fellows. It almost breaks my heart when I think of you and them and cannot see you all nor hear from you all.

*But I put my trust in the Lord. And I
hope and pray to the Almighty that
the time may soon come that we may
meet hand and hand and heart and heart.*

*Ann, I often times think of the
times that I have misspent heretofore.
But I hope and pray to God that we
may both be engaged in his holy works
from this time on. I must close for
this time by sending my love to you
and Der little children and to all
inquiring friends and to all my
Brethren in the Lord. Tell them to
remember me in all their prayers So
nothing more but remaining your
affectionate companion until death.*

Henry Garst to Ann Garst

[Spelling and punctuation in letter have been corrected to make it easier to read.]

On the back of his letter, Henry had added two
notes. One said that Ann's brother Abraham was in
Clark County, Ohio, and was well a short time ago.

The second note gave new directions for mailing
letters to him.

Nathan smiled when his mama read *"Der* little
children." *Der* was the German word for "the."
Nathan knew Papa had learned to read and write
German before he learned to read and write

English. Sometimes he mixed the two languages in his writing. Occasionally he also did that when he spoke, Nathan remembered fondly.

"Poor Papa. He misses us so much," Mama said. "What a pity that he didn't get the letters we wrote. We must write to him again and use the new mailing instructions that he gave us."

And that is just what they did. As soon as Grandma and Grandpa had gone, Mama and Nathan both wrote letters. Marshall wrote some letters of the alphabet on a piece of paper and printed his name. Even Monroe made a few scratches on paper. "Papa. Letter," he babbled happily.

"Do you think Monroe remembers Papa?" Nathan asked his mama.

"I doubt if he really remembers him," Mama responded. "But when he hears us talk about Papa, I think he knows that he is someone we love and who loves us, too."

CHAPTER 8

Peacemaking Begins

 It was almost spring again. School closed early. Very few men were left in the community, and the children were needed to help the women plant gardens and crops.

The Garst family was planting potatoes. Ann prepared the seed by cutting last year's potatoes into several pieces, making sure there was an eye to sprout in each piece.

Nathan was a tall lad and strong for his eleven years. He could do most of the work that a man usually did. Today Nathan made long rows with the plow and horse. Ann carried a large basket of the cut potatoes. She walked along behind Nathan and dropped the potato pieces into one of the rows. Marshall walked beside his mother, dropping pieces into another row. From time to time, Ann checked to be sure that the small boy did not drop the pieces too far apart or too close together. She also kept an eye on Monroe, who played at the edge of the potato patch.

When a row was filled with potato pieces, Nathan made another pass with the plow to carefully push dirt over the seed potatoes.

After the potatoes were planted, Nathan spent most of each day preparing the red clay soil for other crops. Sometimes as he followed the plow, he thought of Papa. He remembered how he used to follow Papa in the fields when he was very small. He recalled how Papa sometimes let him ride one of the horses from the field back to the barn.

I wonder if Papa is planting crops in Illinois, Nathan thought.

In Illinois, Henry Garst was working each day in the fields. He was glad to help the Brethren farmers who had opened their homes to the Virginia Brethren when they fled the South. But as he tilled the fields, he thought about his family.

He thought about the letters he had received from home. Nathan assured him that he could manage the plowing. And Ann praised their oldest son for his ability and his hard work. Still, Henry thought, a father should be there to provide for his family. He felt guilty about being so far away.

As he worked the rich, black Illinois soil, he prayed for his family. He prayed that the time would soon come when he could return to them.

And as he prayed, the words of David in the Bible came to his mind.

He delivered me from my strong enemy,
and from them that hated me:
for they were too strong for me.
They prevented me in the day of my
calamity: but the Lord was my stay.
He brought me forth also into a large
place: He delivered me, because he
delighted in me. (2 Sam. 22:18-20)

Henry felt sure that God had led him to Illinois to deliver him from his enemies. He believed that some day God would lead him back again. He prayed that the day would come soon when nations would "beat their swords into plowshares, and their spears into pruning hooks" and that nations would "learn war no more" (Isa. 2:4).

Henry promised God that he would walk in the ways of the Lord and follow him forever.

Back in the Greenridge community, there were frequent reports on the progress of the war. For those loyal to the Confederacy, the news was mostly bad.

Union General Sherman and his army had marched down through Georgia, defeating the Southern forces and ruthlessly destroying farms and cities. Now he was leading his troops up through North Carolina toward Richmond, Virginia. There General Grant had been attacking the Confederate army led by General Lee.

The Union forces greatly outnumbered the Southern armies. The Southern soldiers were poorly fed, poorly clothed, and short of supplies. The situation was so desperate that Confederate President Jefferson Davis fled Richmond.

On April 10, Ann and Nathan were planting corn when Greta Speagle rode up on horseback. She had just come from Salem where she had learned the latest news.

"Yesterday General Lee surrendered to General Grant at Appomattox," she reported. "The church bells in Salem tolled each time a Salem soldier died in battle," she recalled. "Today the slow sorrowful notes of the bells are announcing the death of the Southern cause. The Confederacy has lost the war."

After Greta left, Nathan looked at his mama. "I know Brethren meetinghouses don't have bells," he said, "but if our meetinghouse did have a bell, I think it would announce the end of the war with a joyful noise." Ann agreed with her son.

Then Nathan added, "The war won't really be over for us until Papa comes home."

Soldiers began to return home. Some were sick or wounded. All were hungry, ragged, and weary. Among those returning were James and Elias Garst.

Nathan was glad for his uncles and the other soldiers who returned safely to their families But his mind was filled with one burning question: When will Papa come home? He asked his mama. He asked his grandpa. He asked the elders at Sunday meeting. Everyone replied, "Soon, I hope." But nobody could really answer his question.

So Nathan kept on hoping and working. He wanted the farm to be in good shape when Papa did return.

❋ ❋ ❋ ❋ ❋

Kurt Weber had recovered from his war injuries. With his new wooden leg, he was able to do many kinds of work around the farm. Some people were still not friendly to him. But now that the war was over, he was free to come and go as he pleased.

One fine spring day, Kurt decided to go to Fincastle. Some of the corn he and Martin planted had not come up. He had not been able to find more seed. Someone told him that a farm store in Fincastle had seed corn. He might find other things there that he needed, too. So he decided to take the wagon instead of going on horseback.

Kurt found the seed and other supplies at the store. As he was leaving the building, he heard a voice that sounded strangely familiar. It seemed like he had heard this voice before, but he couldn't remember when or where. He had a fleeting but strong feeling that the voice was important to him in some way. He turned and looked at the men in the store but saw no familiar face, so he started toward his wagon.

The storekeeper called out to Kurt. "Did you say you live near Salem? There's a man here looking for a ride to that area."

Kurt went back into the store. "Kurt Weber," he said, extending his hand to the stranger who was seeking a ride.

"Henry Garst," the stranger replied. Kurt was startled and puzzled. It was the oddly familiar voice. Kurt recognized the name at once. But he couldn't remember ever having met Henry Garst before now.

The two men shook hands. Then Kurt spoke again. "I know your family, and I have heard about you. I am Greta Speagle's brother."

"I'm glad that you could come and visit Greta now that the war is over," Henry said. "Friedrick's death was very hard for her."

"I'm not visiting my sister," Kurt explained. "I'm living with her and the children now. I was with the Union cavalry at Hanging Rock. That's where I lost my leg. When they were getting ready to move all the Union soldiers from the Dunkard church, I requested permission to stay with my sister's family. It was not easy, but finally I got permission to stay."

Henry looked at Kurt. He remembered that battle. He remembered the wounded man he found in the woods and took to the meetinghouse. He had been so busy tending the man's wound that he had not really looked into his face while the torch was lit. Could this be the same man?

Kurt interrupted Henry's thoughts. "It was lucky that I did not lose my life as well as my leg. After I was shot, my horse carried me far into the woods on the mountainside. Someone found me there late at night. He bandaged my leg and took me to the church. No one knew who brought me there."

"I am the one who found you!" Henry said.

"Of course!" Kurt replied. "That's why your voice is so familiar. Since I first heard you speak at the store, I've been trying to remember where I heard that voice."

"You didn't hear it for long. You told me about the runaway horse and then passed out."

"I'm confused. Weren't you in Illinois during the war?" Kurt asked. "Ann spoke of your absence and your beliefs."

"I didn't leave Virginia until the fall of 1864. I was hiding in the woods on the mountainside during the battle of Hanging Rock. That's where I found you."

Kurt was silent for a while. Then he spoke. "It must have been very dangerous for you to take me to the church. That's why no one would tell me how I got there. You risked your life to save mine."

"Only one person saw me there that night, and he was a friend," said Henry. He told no one but Ann and Nathan. I see they kept the secret well."

As they continued their trip, the two men talked about the war. Henry explained his belief that all war is wrong. He could not kill or harm another human. And he could not help others fight. That is why he finally had to leave his family and flee to Illinois. Now he was making his way back home.

Kurt told Henry that he had joined the Union army because he thought slavery was wrong. He described some of the battles in which he had fought. "I still think slavery is wrong," the younger man said. "But there must have been another way to end it," he added sadly.

On that point the two men agreed.

When they reached Greenridge, Kurt drove Henry to his home. He would not go inside with him. He thought Henry would want to greet his family alone.

As they approached the farm, Kurt noticed Nathan working in a field behind the barn. While Henry went inside, Kurt tied his horses to a tree and went to get the boy. Nathan was surprised to see him.

"I just got back from Fincastle," Kurt told him. "I brought a surprise for you, and I couldn't wait for you to see it."

"Can't it wait until I finish here?" Nathan wanted to know.

"No," Kurt answered. "You must come with me to your house right now."

The door to the house was open. As Nathan entered, Kurt slipped quietly away to his wagon and returned home.

Inside the house Nathan saw Mama, his brothers, and— "PAPA!" he shouted. "You're home."

Henry put his hands on Nathan's shoulders and looked at him. He didn't say, "How you've grown." In fact he didn't say anything. He just pulled his son close and held him. It was Nathan who spoke first. "NOW the war is over!" he exclaimed.

For a long time the family talked. They talked about Henry's long trip home from Illinois. They talked about the farm and the crops. They talked about how they had missed each other. But mostly they talked about how good it was to be together again.

The sun was low in the sky when there was a knock at the door. It was Martin with a big pot of stew.

"Mama sent you this stew, Mrs. Garst. She said you'd be too excited to cook," Martin said to Ann.

Then Martin went over to Henry. "I'm glad you're home," he said, extending his hand. "And I sure thank you for saving Uncle Kurt's life."

Then Martin turned to Nathan. "Mama said I could help you with your evening chores. She said she reckoned you hadn't had time to think about them yet."

"She's right," Nathan admitted. "But let's do them now. It won't take long with your help."

As the boys went out the door arm in arm, Martin said to Nathan, "Your papa is one brave man."

"Yes, the war is truly over," Ann said, nodding toward the boys, "and peacemaking has begun."

POSTSCRIPT

Would you like to know what happened after the story ended?

Henry and Ann Garst continued to farm their land in the Greenridge area of Roanoke County. After the war, they had four more children—two girls and two boys.

Henry and Ann were "engaged in holy works" just as Henry had hoped in the letter printed in the story. Henry became a minister and elder at the Peters Creek meetinghouse, and Ann helped him in his work.

Jeremiah Garst, Henry's younger brother who was with him in Illinois, also became a minister and elder there. And so did Nathan when he grew up.

The Peters Creek church building is much bigger now than in 1865, and it is no longer called a meetinghouse. But that original meetinghouse is a part of the present day church building.

—*N.G.P.*